Keely

By
D. Alan Lewis

Keely

Published by D. Alan Lewis and
Voodoo Rumors Media

Interior by D. Alan Lewis
Edited by Susan Burdorf

Voodoo Rumors Media
Nashville, Tennessee 37211

Acknowledgements

Keely is the result of an idea I had while putting together the steampunk/superhero anthology, *Capes & Clockwork: Superheroes in the Age of Steam* for Dark Oak Press.

That book, released in early 2014, helped spur on my love of steampunk and the cross-blending of that genre with the action and pulp-styled stories of superheroes.

While putting that anthology together, the original Keely story was drastically shortened. I am happy that I can finally tell the whole story in this volume

While Keely in the story isn't real, her name comes from a friend who graciously agreed to lend it to me for the tale. Therefore, to the real Keely, I say Thank you.

Chapter 1

She fell from the sky without fanfare or notice by the few inhabitants that still called this God-forsaken city home. I doubt that anyone, save the four of us who stood near the impact point, witnessed the event that was to change everything. Her youthful form dropped through the black fog that hung over the city. She hit with such force that cobblestones for a dozen feet around her went to powder.

Dodging the debris and dust that arose and then fell like rain around her, I approached. The stonework of Warner Place had opened up from the strike and now cradled the young woman like a babe in its mother's arms. Her nude form lay completely still and I strained to see if her lungs took in breath. As a man in my thirties, I'd seen nude women many times, but I felt awkward looking at her. I felt that my concentration on her chest would give others pause to speculate as to my intentions. Her chest didn't rise as if breaths were drawn and that brought on a profound sense of loss. Only her long blond hair moved, dancing in the wind.

"Did ya see that?" an old woman said as she stepped up to my side. "A bit unseemly, I'd say. Guess she flung herself off the roof. Another jumper I reckon." She scoffed when my eyes didn't move away from the young woman. "Could've had the decency to put a stitch or two on before leaping."

I glanced at her and nodded slightly. An elderly couple braved the dust as well to get a look at her. While the old man studied the scene intently, his wife tugged at his arm, not wanting to see what she assumed was a tragedy. She nagged him to take her home until he finally gave in. They walked off without another word spoken.

The number of folks who'd jumped from the rooftop, or taken their own lives by other means, had steadily increased after the European continent had formally collapsed and fallen into the hands of the Otherworlders. The number increased even more when word reached us that the Americans had fallen as well.

With England now standing alone against the alien horde, many of our people had lost hope and now only longed for a quick, painless end. I couldn't blame them. The skies had turned dark, which mirrored the mood in our nation. Defeat had fallen on every attempt our army and navy had made against the enemy. Everyone knew it was just a matter of time before the shores of our isle were tarnished with their boot prints.

The Otherworlders wanted more than just land, they wanted us. Every captured soul in the occupied lands was nothing more than food stock, assuming that anyone other than the aliens still lived in those blackened lands. London stood almost empty due to the daily bombing that rained in each afternoon from the massive cannons on the northern coast of France.

My gaze moved to the rooftops. I scanned for any signs of foul play. A naked girl just doesn't fall from the sky, but what bothered me were the heights of the surrounding structures. The buildings were simply not tall enough for someone to have achieved the speed necessary to make such a devastating impact. When my eyes returned to her, I lacked the ability to understand why her body didn't show more signs of damage or distress. The impact should have shattered her petite form, spilling blood and organs everywhere.

But she lay there looking as beautiful as a sleeping princess. All she needed was a prince to kiss and awaken her to fulfill the fairytale. Flawless, pale flesh, and golden locks were a stark contrast to the dark, crumbled stones she lay in, like a gleaming white pearl resting within the black and gray shell of an oyster.

"I don't think she jumped," I whispered, only to hear the old woman scoff again.

Cautiously, I stepped into the crater and knelt beside her. Her chest moved slightly, and I almost jumped. Truth be told, my heart froze and my body jerked nervously. Clearing my throat, I looked back to the old woman.

"She's alive. She's breathing," my voice shook slightly, hinting at the fear within me. I knew she couldn't be natural, maybe not even of this world. No human could have survived a fall like that. I inwardly cursed my inability to deal with the moment in a calm and professional manner.

"She… she must be hurt. Is… is there a carriage about?" I said in a broken, stuttering manner.

"Bloomin' city is emptied out. Ain't nobody around here exceptin' you and me," the woman said, sarcastically.

My mind raced as I tried to decide what course of action would be best. Surely she needed help, medical attention and what not, but without a cart, that meant carrying the lass a dozen or so blocks to the nearest hospital. My flat lay just around the corner, but, I wasn't a doctor, not in the medical sense, anyway. And there was the meeting that I should already be sitting at.

I had hoped to catch one of the few remaining steambuses that still managed to operate in this war-torn metropolis in order to get to Whitehall and the War Office. My meeting wasn't urgent, it was more of the usual updating the Admiralty on my efforts thus far with my latest weapon. I'm a scientist, a tinkerer, and since the war started, a reluctant weapons designer. As a child, my gifts for science and technology were fostered by my mother, but she pressed her Christian morality on me as well. Fighting and killing were not within my nature. Before the stars fell, my inventions were meant to help mankind. Now, I had to battle my own convictions and tell myself that my inventions were meant to help mankind by keeping it in existence.

I started to scoop her into my arms but hesitated. It'd be unseemly to carry a nude young woman about town, let alone into my flat. I glanced at the old woman and caught sight of a flagpole behind her. The impact had damaged the stones beneath it, causing it to tilt over at a low angle. I bolted over to it, snatched the Union Jack that dangled from its midpoint and returned to the crater. With care, I wrapped her up and then lifted the unconscious woman from the damaged stones.

The young woman's body felt limp in my arms. I

groaned at the weight, estimating her at fourteen stone. Yet, she was a tiny little thing and appeared to weigh half that amount. It didn't make sense. My muscles strained and I had to adjust my hold a few times until I could stand and carry her from her crater. I moved slowly, dodging the broken stones and debris. I feared tripping and dropping her, yet the idea struck me as amusing. She'd fallen from the sky, I'm sure she'd survive a fall from this height. But looking at her round face, I couldn't allow her to fall again.

"Whatchya gonna do?" the old woman yelled.

I stopped and thought, not really knowing what the best course of action would be. Looking back, I replied, "Taking her home. My woman can see to her needs while I fetch a doctor."

Then I remembered the situation at home. I had no woman or servants of any kind, not any more. My housekeeper had abandoned me and the city after the enemy's shells began to fall. All that awaited us in my flat was a laboratory and enough food for maybe a month of good eating. Still, there were few options and her weight prohibited me from carrying her all the way to the hospital.

"On second thought, my woman... my housekeeper has escaped the city. Perhaps, you could assist?" I asked. "I'm lousy when it comes to cooking and I'm sure she needs a meal and what-not. Besides, she may be injured, and I'll need a caretaker for her."

She looked annoyed until I mentioned food. "Well, mind ya that I'm only coming along causin' it wouldn't be proper for a man your age to be carrying a girl like that about."

"I have others at the lab, several men who assist me in my work, but they'd be no help with…' I said, nodding toward the woman in my arms.

As I did so, my eyes fixated on the beauty of her face. Without a doubt, her beauty was beyond measure. She had rich full lips that were as red as crimson and a small nose which turned up slightly at the tip. My thoughts were so dazzled by her appearance that I failed to see anything else, including the old woman as she approached from behind. She stepped quickly to my side and gave me a suspicious look.

"Call me Mattie."

I nodded and glanced over at her, "Umm—and I am Thomas Laybourne, the third. My friends call me Tom."

"Hmm, nice to be makin' your acquaintance, Mr. Laybourne."

As we reached my flat, a lamplighter tilted his hat and started up his ladder. He glanced back down at us once the coal gas in the lantern was aflame. The warm yellow glow fell on the sidewalk, reminding me of better times.

"I know it's only two-ish, but they're saying it's gonna be a particularly dark one, this day. Word is that more blackness is rolling in over the channel," he said and climbed down.

Tilting my head back, I spied the black clouds that rolled and churned overhead. These weren't storm clouds bringing in the much-needed rain to our lands. No one knew for certain what kind of gases floated in our skies nowadays or what their purpose was. We only knew that the Otherworlders created the clouds for their own diabolical reasons.

High-flying airships had traversed the darkness, only to fall back to earth hours later, their crew's dead. The poisons in the atmosphere soaked through their clothing, staining their skin black. Medical examinations proved that their lungs were darker than that of coal miners who'd lived a lifetime underground. The poor devils in those ships never had a chance. A Royal Institute of Science airship, commanded by the Air Navy made an attempt to study the clouds using the latest gasmasks and chemical suits. The poisons found a weak point on each crewman's suit, killing them with impunity. After that, no more attempts were made to study the clouds and warnings were sent out for all air vessels to stay well below the cloud-base.

"Never thought I'd be complainin' 'bout the sun. That fireball always was too bright for these old eyes, but I'd like ta see it again," Mattie said, looking skyward with moist eyes.

"Me too," I said, longing for the familiar warmth of the sun on my face.

"Damn them slugs. Hope they all burn in hell," Mattie muttered.

The government called them Otherworlders, but most people called them slugs due to their thick, slimy bodies. They first appeared, or landed, in the Russian frontier. In short order, they conquered and claimed those cold lands as their own. No one was certain how they built the first smoke factory. Some, like myself, thought the first ships may have contained small factories within them. Whatever the truth was, they began pumping out a seemingly endless torrent of thick black smoke. As additional ships arrived from whatever world they left behind, more and larger smoke factories sprang up. With all of Europe, Asia, Africa, and the Americas under their thumbs, hundreds of factories kept adding to the thick layer that already engulfed most of the Earth.

"Let's get her inside," I said and climbed the six steps to my front door.

Mattie nodded to the building next to mine. "Why would ya be wanting to live here? A terrace house nestled up close to a factory?"

A short laugh escaped me, "Factory? No, no. That's my laboratory."

Chapter 2

My flat would never win awards from the women who used to run the local neighborhood societies. Its décor showed all the attributes of bachelorhood. Dishes lay everywhere and not enough attention to cleaning had allowed a light coating of dust to form on every unused surface.

I carried her upstairs to my guest bedroom, with Mattie in tow. As we entered, I nodded to the bed. She caught my meaning and pulled the linens back as I lay the young woman down.

"Mattie, if you'll remain here at her side, I'll fetch a doctor," I said, but then hesitated. Something about her just kept me in place. My hand reached for hers as I sat beside her. My attention shifted away from her briefly as I turned to the old woman. I felt panicked at the thought of being away from her which I found hard to explain since I didn't even know the woman. "On second thought, would you please fetch the doctor? My friend Percy Hunter lives nearby. He has some medical training. I can give you the address." With a nod, she answered, "Ole man

Hunter? I've known him for a long while. You don't has to tell me where he's at. When I get back with him, I'll be inspecting that kitchen of yours and fixing meself a decent meal." She glanced back and forth between the young woman and me. "Can I trust you to be a decent gentleman while I'm gone?"

"Of course, she'll come to no harm or exploitation in your absence." I answered, understanding her concern but slightly annoyed by it as well.

I walked Mattie to the front door, handing her two pence as we descended the interior stairs. When the front door opened, the soft droning of propellers could be heard. She seemed excited and bolted into the street and scanned the sky. I followed suit and kept my eyes over the rooftops to the north. Within short order, six airships appeared below the blackened clouds. The silvery gray of their skin, along with the brilliance of their running lights' made the vivid colors of the Union Jacks and other signaling banners stand out.

"Beautiful, ain't they?" she said, never looking away from the majestic sight of the floating warships. "Look at 'em. Who'd thought a few years ago that they'd even have been built, let alone be our only salvation from the slugs. God bless the blokes that made 'em."

"Thank you, Mattie," I said and saw her shoot me a crooked glance. I waved to my laboratory and workshop behind us. "I designed much of their systems for the War Office. That's what I do and why I'm still in London. I'm a weapons and munitions designer. The first engine prototype used on those ships was built and tested thirty feet from where we're standing. The big guns and the explosive bombs, all found life on my design tables."

She looked me up and down, as if seeing me for the first time. "Well, ain't life just full of surprises today?" We turned and watched the airships disappear over the rooftops. "Hope those lads bomb them slugs real good. Be nice to have some good news from the front, for a change."

"I'm curious. The government ordered the civilian and nonessential folks to clear out of the city. So...."

"Are you sayin' I'm not essential?" she said and shook her head. "I've been in London all me life and I'm not lettin' any slug or royal tell me to go. Besides, I got no place outside of here, so I reckon I'm here till the end. And I ain't alone. Lots of us around here aren't gonna pack up."

A thought struck me and I drew my pocket watch to check the time.

"You better hurry," I said and snapped the watch's cover closed. "Almost two. The shelling will start up in an hour or so. And wrap that scarf around a second time. The clouds are going to thicken later, so the temperature will drop lower."

"Here's hopin' we ain't gonna have snow dropping on us again, like last week," Mattie complained and adjusted her collar. "I remember when June was supposed to be a warm summer month."

"It helps them," I said and saw her squint an eye at me. "The slugs seem to function better in the cold. That's why they built the smoke factories, I think. They mean to blot out the sun and bring an everlasting winter to our world. No sun. No warmth."

I didn't want to induce the same fear within her that had already paralyzed much of the government. Without the sun, plant life would die off and in doing so, humanity's food sources would wither away. We were on course to lose the war, not because of their advanced weapons, but from starvation and exposure. The prospect was a truly hellish way for humanity to end, cold and hungry.

She nodded and scurried off. I prayed that she and the doctor would return before the daily attack began. The droning of more propellers made me look up. A solitary airship passed overhead, following the fleet we'd watched earlier. I silently thanked God that at least we controlled the sky.

After the Otherworlders began their advance across Europe, it seemed that the British would fall as easily as every other nation. But by God's grace, our nation exploited the one weakness they hadn't expected, weight.

When the first reports came back from the fronts, observers saw what could only have been heavier then air flying vehicles. The slugs appeared to know the secrets of flight, but the gravity of our world must be far greater than theirs. Their aircraft couldn't fly because they couldn't overcome Earth's constant pull. But their miscalculation in weight gave us other advantages as well.

Although huge and bulky, their strength was diminished. On their home world, I could only imagine that they wielded physical strengths that would match the tales of the gods of Olympus. Their land rovers, giant armored vessels sitting atop eight wheels and bristling with cannons, criss-crossed the lands. Just one such vehicle could, given time, lay waste to an entire city. But their size and weight made it all but impossible to transport over water. It was another favor that God had blessed the British Isles with, a suitable stretch of water to protect and isolate us.

ભ્ભ૭૭ભ્ર૭

I returned to the side of the mysterious woman, but her condition hadn't changed in the short time I'd been away. She lay there, a goddess swaddled in cotton linens. I lifted her hand and immediately felt worried at the lack of warmth. She still drew breath, but that was all. I couldn't see any other sign of life. Nothing but the slow rise and fall of her chest even hinted at life. I snatched a chair away from its home next to the writing desk and sat beside her.

Time seemed to slip away from me as my fingers toyed with her hair. A blast shook the building. A glance to the window confirmed my suspicions as smoke, marbled with vivid oranges and reds, bloomed upwards over the nearby buildings. The shelling, a daily fixture in the lives of Londoners, had renewed as it did at 3pm each afternoon. I leaned over her, protecting her face from the light sprinkling of plaster dust that each blast jarred loose from the ceiling and walls.

The exploding metal rained down upon the city for half an hour then ceased. Stepping to the window, I surveyed the damage to my abandoned metropolis. When the Otherworlders began the shelling, the government called for a partial evacuation. Each day the shells fell on London and drove more and more people away to the safety of the countryside. Their shells were small and did little damage. A single one couldn't destroy a building, but it could ignite a fire that would consume not just it, but an entire city block.

I stayed with her, brushing her hair with my fingers, and wondering who this goddess was and where she'd come from. As my fingers pushed the blond locks back, something unusual caught my eye. Her ears weren't rounded on top but instead came to a point. My first thought was of the stories of old, myths and legends of pointy-eared elves.

As I rolled her head slightly to get a better look, a short moan escaped her lips. I froze momentarily but relaxed when I saw that she remained unconscious. My heartbeat again and a sudden feeling of loneliness fell upon me. This beauty remained lost to me, and my unexpected need for her company tugged at something deep and primal inside me.

Laying her hand down, I stood, stretched, and moved across the bedroom to the windows. The darkness in the room was deeper than outside, so I pulled open the thick drapes on both windows to even it out.

Smoke rose from a few spots in the city where fires raged from the shelling. The black clouds shifted somewhat, allowing thin slivers of sunlight to break through and fall like rain upon my city. The rays moved with the clouds, illuminating an area for a moment before moving on to another. Some rays lasted minutes while others disappeared almost as quickly as they appeared. It was a sad sight and at the same time, a beautiful one. Since the smoke appeared, the sun had not bathed London in her warm light for more than a few minutes and never in its entirety. It reminded me of the struggle at hand, darkness consuming us, but the human spirit refusing to submit and breaking through the Otherworlders' claim to this world in shimmering blasts of vibrant, albeit brief, rays of illuminated energy.

A ray fell upon my window and the warmth was welcome on my skin. I moved to the side, then drew the curtains open wide so that it filled the room and fell upon her. Her face seemed to glow as the yellowish light washed over her. I lost myself in the serenity of the scene until she inhaled sharply and sat straight up. Her look of fear and confusion had to match my startled expression.

She pushed herself back against the headboard and looked around the room. Her eyes darted around taking in the details and finally settling on me. Those beautiful green eyes narrowed in suspicion and she began talking, loud at first but softening up as she went.

The language she spoke was lost on me. I knew French, German and Russian but this sounded like none of them. I'd grown up here and spent my childhood running about in the streets of London. I was used to hearing strange dialects from visitors from every corner of the globe. A word here and there from all these languages had stuck with me, and yet, her words were alien to me.

I started to put my hand up to stop her but stopped myself. Her voice was beautiful, feminine and her dialect had a lyrical quality like the French language, only sweeter, if that were possible. She seemed to sing the words instead of speaking them.

When I didn't respond, she stopped and stared. Deciding this was my opportunity; I raised my hands to show I meant no harm and stepped forward.

"I'm not going to hurt you," I said and watched her face scrunch up in confusion. Another route was needed. I placed my right hand on my chest and said, "Thomas Laybourne." The name was repeated several times before she nodded in understanding.

She pointed a finger at me and tried a few times until she pronounced my name correctly. "Thomas Laybourne." When I nodded, she warmed the room with her smile. Then she placed a hand on her chest, barely covered by the blue sheets and gave me her name. "Keely."

"I'm pleased to meet you, Keely," I replied and looked around the room trying to decide what the hell I was going to do now.

Chapter 3

"And you say that she just dropped onto the cobblestones?" Percy Hunter asked as we leaned against the wall in the dining room. Keely sat at the table, swaddled in a bed sheet, furiously eating the eggs and bacon Mattie had prepared.

"Fell is putting it mildly," I said and explained the destruction to the street her fall had produced. Glancing at her plate, I added, "She has quite the appetite. Mattie, can you fix another plate for Keely? And while you're at it, fix enough for all of us, please?"

Dr. Hunter stepped to the table and sat across from the young woman. She looked up at him and stopped eating. When I sat beside him and gave her a reassuring smile, she returned to the meal. Our gazes remained fixated on her as she quickly ate and muttered something adorable in her native language. "Tom, I don't recognize it at all," Hunter said and pulled out a note pad to jot some thoughts down. "And the ears are pointed you say?" I nodded and he continued. "And you say she was nude at the time of impact?"

Mattie appeared from the kitchen with another plate. "Girl didn't have a stitch on and if yous ask me, something oughta be done about that first thing." She replaced Keely's plate with a full one and looked at us. "Not very proper having a naked young thing like her romping around your house in nothing but bedclothes with you menfolk ogling her. After she's done eatin, I'll fetch one of your nightshirts for her to wear. Assuming you have anything clean enough for a lady to wear."

I shifted uncomfortably, "Yes, well ... I don't keep a supply of women's garments lying about. And my shirts should do fine, although laundry isn't a priority these days, so I can't promise the cleanliness will be to your liking. Perhaps you can provide something for our guest?" I watched the woman's eyebrows rise in mock defiance. "And since you've expressed your concerns so clearly, I'd like for you to remain here with us, for the time being... to help out with the cooking and care for..." I waved a hand at Keely. "And of course, I'll ensure you're well paid for your efforts and you'd have full reign of the pantry."

"Well, since you put it so nice like..." Mattie scoffed and left only to return in short order with a plate for each of us. She took a seat next to Keely and began eating.

"How old do you think she is?" I asked and watched him look her up and down.

"Twenty, give or take a couple of years. Of course, I'm talking human years. No telling in a case like this." Hunter replied.

I nodded in agreement. "I just don't know about her. She's like an angel fallen from on high."

"Aside from the ears," Hunter said as he inspected his eggs with his fork. "Did you see any other physiological differences with her body?" He glanced over at me and saw my discomfort. "After all, she was nude; surely you looked her over for damage from the fall."

"I did not. In all other aspects, she appears as normal as you and I."

"Very well then, I'll give the girl a proper inspection after we eat," Hunter said in a nonchalant manner.

Seeing Mattie's demeanor change as if she were coiling up like a snake and preparing to strike, I added, "And to assure peace of mind to the ladies, I'd suggest that Mattie assist."

Hunter looked at both women and cleared his throat, "Right. Of course."

"I'll be back to look in on her in the morning," Dr. Hunter said as he stepped out the front door. He turned back to me with an expression of confusion, mirroring my own. "She appears perfectly human, except for the ears. And her skin…" He paused and we both remembered the myriad of times and ways he'd attempted to extract blood only to have each needle snap rather than puncture her skin. "My boy, there must be an explanation for her and her abrupt appearance." He began walking but turned around and joking added, "Of course, if young beauties such as her are going to start randomly dropping from the sky, perhaps that'll encourage me to spend less time in the lab and more time walking about."

Mattie stepped into the doorway behind me and pushed by. "Begging your pardon, but I'm going to skip my way home. I'll be back in the morning with my things since I'll be staying with you and the young woman."

"Of course, Mattie," I said and stepped back into the flat.

"I expect you to behave yourself around her this evening or do I need to come back tonight?"

I couldn't help but laugh, "Of course. She'll be perfectly safe. By the way, how far is your home?"

"I live down the road over me shoppe," she responded. "Warner's Dressmakers."

"You're a seamstress? Perhaps you have…"

She scoffed, "Yes, yes. I'll bring the girl some proper clothes instead of your dingy old shirts to wear about."

Keely stepped up behind me, laid a hand on my shoulder and peered out at Mattie. Her touch was electric. We stood and watched the old woman walk out of sight and then I glanced back at Keely. Her gaze moved to and fro, studying the cityscape. Like a fool, it only then struck me that she'd never seen London.

"If you like this, you'll love the roof," I said, took her hand, and led her to my bedroom.

The window was thrown open and I carefully crawled out onto the rooftop. I reached in and took her hand to steady her as she climbed through to join me. We slowly moved to the top. I sat and patted the clay tiles next to me. She sat and nuzzled herself against me to keep warm. Again, like a fool, I'd forgotten how bitterly cold the city was, especially at night and she wore only a thin shirt that Mattie had found for her and still had the sheet wrapped around her waist. I put an arm around her and pulled her close.

"There. You can see Big Ben," I said and pointed to the distant tower. "And over there. Do you see that sparkling gray ribbon partially hidden behind the buildings? That's the Thames. "

She tilted her head against my arm and followed the direction of my finger, gazing out at the city. One by one, I pointed out all the visible landmarks. Her arms wrapped around me and squeezed affectionately. The closer she pushed into me, the stronger her scent became. I tilted my head and caught a scent from her hair. I couldn't identify the smell, but it was sweet and intoxicating. I knew that if we remained this close, I'd not be able to pull away.

"Are you cold?" I asked.

Noting her trembling lips and the goose bumps on her shivering legs, I took that as confirmation that she was. We returned to my bedroom and from there, I led her to the guest room where she'd awakened earlier. I patted the bed and like a little girl, she jumped onto it and sat looking at me.

With some effort, I convinced her to lie down. She scowled and sat up, pulling the shirt and sheet off. I glanced away, feeling I wasn't keeping to my agreement with Mattie. Keely lay back down and I pulled the sheets over her but she kept pulling them down. She looked at me with eyes wide open and an expression of innocence. Nudity must be the norm wherever it was she came from.

"I don't know how to explain this to you," I said gently. "Around here, on this world, we wear

26

clothing. It keeps us warm and protects us from…"

I shook my head and realized that none of it was getting through. The pillows were snatched up, fluffed and put back into place. It took a little time, but I finally got Keely to lie down. In short order, the young woman was asleep.

I stepped to the door and turned off the electric lights that illuminated the room. Earlier that afternoon, the shelling had ignited a fire in an abandoned hotel several blocks away. While the firefighters had contained the inferno to just the one structure, the flames rose up high into the night sky from the roof. Its flickering light filled the room with a warm glow. I looked at her, lying in the bed, looking so peaceful as she slept.

Again, the nagging questions loomed in the forefront of my mind.

What am I going to do now? Who is she and where is she from?

Chapter 4

As the sun rose, I awoke to the sounds of my workers entering the workshop. Glancing over, I saw that the alarm had not sounded on my clock and I'd overslept by an hour. The normal ruckus was a little rowdier than usual this morning, which immediately aroused suspicion. Voices called out and wolf whistles echoed from the rear of my flat.

I was on my feet instantly, recklessly charging down the stairs and out the back door in my nightshirt. Behind my flat and adjoining workshop was an open expanse. The property had originally held three buildings, but when they fell into disrepair, I purchased them and had them removed. Now, the walled-off land was used as a safe place to test some of the equipment I designed.

As I stepped out of my flat, I saw the source of my men's unsavory attention. Keely ran from one side of the field to the next, naked and laughing. The rays of the sun shone down, illuminating patches of soil as they moved across from wall to wall. It was a game to her, chasing the patches of sunlight and bathing herself in it.

"Back to work!" I said. When the six men didn't move fast enough for me, I repeated it in a stronger manner and positioned myself between them and nude woman. "And keep your eyes on your work, not on her."

They reluctantly disappeared back into the workshop as I ran to her. Keely laughed and grabbed my hand. She held to my hand tightly, totally unaware of the compelling image her naked form brought to the minds of my men. She pulled me, against my will, surprising me with her strength, across the field in her game of chasing sunbeams like a children's game of tag. I planted my feet and tried to stop her forward momentum but that only caused me to lose my footing. I fell forward, landing with a loud thud and raising a cloud of dust.

"Oooof!" she exclaimed and then laughed like a girl playing a game. With surprising strength, she pulled me up and hugged me tight.

Surprised, I hugged her back and then realized that something felt wrong. Looking down, I saw that my feet were several inches above the ground, as were hers.

"Whaa…what's happening," I said and then felt the ground as my bare toes touched down on the cold, damp earth. I pushed away from Keely and looked at her smiling, happy face. "Were we just floating?" Her eyes widened as did her smile. I cursed myself for not remembering that she couldn't understand a word I said. And then my gaze moved down, and I remembered why I'd charged out here. "Good Lord, let's get you inside."

Mattie arrived at the front door a short time later and grilled me about the events of the morning. With reluctance, I gave in and explained about Keely's early morning romp around the back yard. Mattie unleashed an angry string of insults and accusation against me, but eventually settled down. But with her moving into the house, I felt that Keely would be safe, not from my interests but from her own naivety.

I led her upstairs where we found Keely standing and bouncing on her bed. It was a bit of a struggle, but we managed to finally get a dress on Keely. It wasn't that she fought us on the idea of putting on the colorful clothing that Mattie had brought. It was that she simply didn't have a clue as to how to put something on. The sleeves were alien to her, and it took a few minutes to get the clothing adjusted to the right arm with the right sleeve. Once this was completed though, she looked down at the foreign fabric covering her body with amusement.

By the time Dr. Hunter arrived and joined us at the table for a quick breakfast she had gotten used to the feel of the material against her skin and, other than a few shoulder movements to drape the clothing on her frame, she seemed to accept that she had to keep them on. At least, until she ripped the sleeves off, leaving her arms bare. For a moment, I thought Mattie was going to faint as she held the ripped sleeves.

"Gonna try and put a corset on her next?" I asked playfully only to get a groan from a very disheveled Mattie who had borne the brunt of trying to get Keely dressed."

"I don't see how that is funny at all," she replied as she placed our plates around the table.

"Mattie, I have to get back to work today. My project requires my attention. Can you keep an eye on Keely?" I asked.

Before she could answer, Dr. Hunter chimed in and said, "My boy, I'll stay here with her. I'm most curious to decipher this language of hers. Besides, with the city mostly empty, I have no patients. They cart all the wounded from the shelling to the local hospitals and well, since my specialty is not surgery, they have little use for me there."

"Seein' as how I'm your unofficial cook and

caretaker, I'll oversee the young woman's care. Not like anyone is coming into buy dresses these days." Mattie said and scoffed at Dr. Hunter. "I don't see why you don't just teach her how to talk proper English."

The doctor and I stopped eating and looked at her as she continued. "Bloody heck, there's a bloomin' schoolhouse a block away from here! I'll walk up there and grab a couple of readers. If you're as smart as you think you are, I'm sure teachin' the girl some basic language skills shouldn't be a problem."

Hunter and I looked at one another, not wanting to admit that we'd not thought of the idea. We nodded and continued eating.

"Are you still working on the same project?" Hunter asked.

"Yes, I should have the detonator ready by next week and the crew should have another month of refining the ores into the exact consistencies we need," I replied.

"Like any of us know what you're talking about," Mattie mumbled.

I laughed a little and said, "The main project the government has me working on is a … well, for the simple explanation, a very powerful bomb." She squinted at me, so I added, "Our airships have had limited success at destroying the smoke factories, but it takes the combined bomb payload of an entire fleet to knock just one out of commission. By the time we're ready to attack a second, they've already repaired the first. This bomb should be powerful enough to wipe out a small city. If our air navy can eradicate the factories along with all of its infrastructure, we may have a chance of turning the tide."

"I read a newspaper report that two more airships were lost yesterday," Hunter said grimly. "Their guns are shooting higher every day. Height is our advantage, but the poisoned clouds give our ships only a finite amount of room left to keep above their range. When we lose that... I just don't know."

Mattie gasped, "I wonder if they were one of those we saw yesterday?"

"I don't know," I replied, sinking back in my seat. I glanced to Keely and watched her smile as she spread a thick layer of butter on her toast. I envied her at that moment, unaware of what the words meant and the distressing news that poured in about the war. I shook my head at the thought; war meant both sides had a chance for victory. This is a struggle for the very survival of our species.

That afternoon, Mattie and Keely returned to the flat after an excursion to the schoolhouse. Their banging and bumping as they entered startled me and I quickly abandoned my reading of the latest reports from the Home Office. Mattie's pale and haggard expression unsettled me as I descended the stairs. I wasn't able to determine if it was fear or shock that twisted the lines of her face in such a disturbing manner. Keely appeared just the opposite, happy and smiling as she carried a large box stacked to the brim with books.

I rushed to Keely and extended my arms, "Oh my dear, let me take those."

She handed the box off to me and I immediately dropped to my knees in an effort to keep from dropping it. Remembering her weight when I carried her home, this box of pulp and binding must have weighed at least twice that amount. With some care, I tried to lower it but it slipped from my hands and landed with a loud thud.

Breathing heavily, I looked up at her and asked, "How did you even get that off the ground?"

Keely's eyes lit up as she leaned down and snatched up the box as if it weighed nothing. She stepped around me and proceeded into the parlor.

I remained there on my knees and pondered what had just happened. How could she have lifted it so easily? I looked to Mattie who wore the same dumbfounded expression that I no doubt did.

"Mattie?" I said but her eyes never left the door to the parlor or the young woman who sat on the couch and drew from the box one book after another.

Keely laughed as she opened each book and found pages of words and colorful drawings. She glanced over and waved for us to join her, but neither of us moved.

"I don't understand. I could barely hold that…" I started but Mattie put me off.

"Ahhh. There is something not right with that girl. If I were a proper Christian, I'd say she were a witch or a demon. Ya should have seen the things I witnessed today."

I slowly pulled myself to my feet, "What did you see?"

The old woman's lips quivered slightly as she spoke. "First off, she were doing her darting about, playing in the sunlight like she always does. But she weren't payin' attention and got out in the middle of the street. One of them bloomin' steambuses came around the corner faster than it oughta and ran straight into her." She paused and took a deep breath, "I ain't making this up, you see … but the whole front of that thing just smashed in around her, like it'd hit a tree. But it weren't no tree, it were her."

I started to laugh, but the seriousness of Mattie's expression stopped me in mid chuckle. She wasn't kidding. I nodded and gave a slight wave to encourage her to continue.

"She just walked away without a scratch. The driver and passengers got off. They were a bit shaken, but I pulled her away and got her to the school as fast as possible. Luckily, all them folks were too shaken to realize what had really happened." I gave Mattie a quizzical look and she added, "I got her away from there. I didn't want her to get into trouble with the law and we don't need a lot of questions floatin' around about her, now do we?"

"You did the right thing. What else happened?"

"Well, we got to the school. The door was locked, and I tugged on it a couple of times. Then she grabbed the knob and yanked it off. That seemed to put her in a mood, so she banged her shoulder against it and the door and facing just shattered. I ain't seen nothing like it. And then she darted about the place faster than I could see. I swear, she moved from room to room so fast, all I could see was a blur."

My mind returned to her morning romp in the back yard, how she'd held me and lifted me off the ground.

"Mattie, just keep an eye on things and speak up if you see any more of these strange occurrences," I whispered. "She's not from around here. We must keep that in mind. And if she is an alien from another world, we have to make sure she is on our side."

An hour later, I stood and looked over the destruction my beautiful young guest had wrought. Just as Mattie had described, the front of the steambus appeared to have caved in, wrapping itself around a young tree or a slender metal post.

"Good Lord, what happened here?" Dr. Hunter said as he stepped up beside me.

I relayed the story that Mattie had shared as well as my own experiences in the backyard and with the box of books.

"Doc, I'm at a loss. This," I waved to the steambus, "has me utterly confounded."

He ran a hand through what little gray hair remained on his head and looked back toward the school.

"Come on, my boy. Let's have a look at that door."

A brisk walk did little to lessen my concerns. When we stepped up to the abandoned school's main entrance, we saw that the door was indeed gone.

Hunter gasped at the devastation to the entryway, "Tom, this door hasn't been knocked down like Mattie said. Look at the splintering. There isn't even a door, only debris. Knocking a door off its hinges would leave it mostly intact. This looks as if a cannonball plowed through."

"Yes," I muttered, "A five foot four, blond cannonball who fell from the sky and really wanted some books."

"With the power that she possesses," Hunter whispered, hinting at a primal fear that festered within both of us. "What happens if we can't control her?"

I slowly nodded, understanding his fear. My expression mirrored his own, "I don't know."

D. Alan Lewis

Chapter 5

The following day, I awoke to find the front door standing wide open and Keely sitting in the doorway, staring out. I moved up behind her and stooped down. The pale green dress, although torn here and there, looked beautiful, although she would have been lovely in sackcloth as well.

"Did you enjoy your walk yesterday with Mattie?" I asked but she said nothing. She looked up at me and the lack of a smile on her face was heartbreaking. I couldn't bear to see her sad and my mind searched for a way to bring the happiness back to her. I was caught up on the day's work and my men could handle the remaining tasks. "Wait, did you want to go back out? For a walk, I mean?"

Again, she looked at me, not understanding my words. I held one hand flat and with the other hand, used my fingers to represent a person walking. When she perked up, I pointed to myself and to her.

"You and I…" I started and then corrected myself. "Thomas and Keely go for a walk through the city?"

She nodded and leapt to her feet. After shoes and jackets were donned, we left and briskly strolled down the avenue, hand in hand. Every shoppe, storefront, and restaurant we passed, grabbed Keely's undivided attention. All the wonders I took for granted were new and exciting to her. She spoke constantly, sometimes to me and other times muttering to herself, but always in her language.

On the few occasions that the sun broke through the clouds, she'd run to touch the rays. On one occasion, she almost tripped over a pair of young boys in her pursuit. A while later, I had to grab her before she stepped into the path of an oncoming steam-powered carriage.

The steambuses raced by us and she paid them no heed. But when the first horse-drawn carriage approached, she jumped behind me, clutching my arms as if she feared the creatures.

"They're just horses," I explained and eased myself to the side to force her to look. "They are large but domesticated. Do you understand? They are work animals."

She looked at me and then jumped out in front of them. The driver pulled hard on the reins and stopped the carriage a few feet in front of her. She stepped a little closer to one of the horses and stared hard at him as the driver shouted obscenities at us.

"Oy, get that lovely outta the road," the driver called.

Keely sniffed at the animals, but they ignored her. She said something and when they didn't respond, she began talking louder.

"Keely!" I exclaimed and she glanced over to me. I stepped closer and took her arm. "Please, step aside, this man has business and we need to let him pass."

She reluctantly moved back onto the sidewalk. The driver smacked the reins down on the animals' hindquarters and the horses began to step forward. Keely immediately stepped forward again, raising a fist in the air and yelling at the driver. I realized that she didn't approve of the driver's use of the leather. I grabbed her arm and stopped her from getting too close.

"So sorry," I shouted up to the driver. "She's new to the city."

We watched the carriage and horses until they were out of sight. Finally, she looked at me, muttered something and proceeded down the sidewalk as if nothing had happened. The entire event would have been comical if it hadn't garnered so much attention from the folks on the surrounding sidewalks.

London may have been mostly evacuated, but

that didn't mean there wasn't still a fair amount in the city. The number of folks remaining in London was somewhere in the tens of thousands. A lot, but nothing like the days before the war began. Most of them were like me, government employees of some make or manner. And it was lunchtime, so most were darting back and forth along the sidewalks, looking for a fresh hot meal. I noticed more people staring at us as we made our way down the debris strewn streets. Keely's rapt interest in everything and everyone we passed was being noticed, and I worried that we were attracting more interest than was necessary. I decided it was time to go back home and took her hand before she could wander away again."

We'd only gotten half a block away when we heard a terrific crash from up ahead. Screams of men and women filled the air. With her hand still in mine, we ran down the street to the intersection. As we approached, others also converged on the scene to see what had caused the commotion.

From what I could deduce, a steambus had rounded the corner too fast and veered off the street. It'd hit a set of steps leading into a townhouse and flipped over. The truly terrible part was that an elderly man lay pinned beneath the contraption. Several men desperately grabbed at the bus in hopes of relieving enough weight so someone else could drag the man out to safety. But their combined efforts were all for naught. The bus was huge, and with its iron boiler and workings combined, the beast must have weighed over ten tons. Only a crane would be able to move the vehicle off the man, and judging by his weakening cries, he did not have that long to wait for rescue.

The gathering crowd watched helplessly as the men struggled and the elderly man clawed at the air, desperately begging for escape. Without hesitation, Keely shook her hand free from mine and ran toward the bus. Just as Mattie had described, she moved so fast that all I saw was a green and gold blur.

Her hands clamped onto the roof of the vehicle and she lifted it with ease. The sight stunned me and brought a collective gasp from the crowd. In fact, they were so startled and ill prepared for the spectacle that no one moved to drag the elderly man to safety.

"Grab his hands and pull him free!" I shouted, pointing to the injured senior.

Two men heard me and reacted quickly, picking him up and moving him away from the wreckage. Once I was sure he was safe, I approached Keely.

"Everyone move away, please!" I shouted again and placed my hand on her shoulder. "Can you push it on over? Set it up right?"

She looked confused but I made some hand

gestures and got my meaning across. She pulled the steambus away from the building, causing the crowd to scatter back. And then she rolled it over onto its tires, righting it easily. She hadn't even raised a sweat, and I did not see her muscles react to the weight of the vehicle.

As the crowd stared at her in shock, I grabbed her hands and pulled her away from it. "We have to go. Come on, we need to go see Mattie and Dr. Hunter."

"Oy, see here. You mind explainin' this?" someone shouted at our backs. Some in the crowd began to follow but we rounded the corner and then ran all the way home so fast that none could follow us as we zigged and zagged between buildings and debris trying to lose them, and succeeding. But I thought later, would we always be able to do that? Surely someone would recognize me eventually. There were not that many people left in London.

CR&OCR&O

"Doc, it was simply incredible," I said, having explained the events.

Mattie, who'd been out shopping that morning, entered the flat with a fearful look. She glanced from Hunter to myself and finally to Keely who sat flipping through her books.

"I reckon all the fuss I'm hearing on the streets is on account of the missy there," she said and point to Keely.

A bad feeling crept up my spine, "What did you hear?"

"Word is out that a young woman lifted a bus and flipped it upright. Saved an old man from a dreadful death. But I think the big news is—she lifted a bus!" Mattie said with a little heat in her tone.

I looked to Hunter. "What … what do you think they could do? I mean, I saw no one there that I recognized. They couldn't know she lives here."

Dr. Hunter stroked the unshaven growth on his chin and moved to sit beside Keely. I noticed him study her for a moment before looking back at me.

"Since you got home, has she done anything?"

"No, nothing but sit and look at her books," I answered but saw concern in his expression.

She looked at him and smiled, but then I saw it too. The vibrant glow of her skin had dissipated. Her complexion had a pale, sickly look about it. And her eyes looked tired, as if she'd not slept well in a week.

Hunter stood and extended his hand to her. She looked up, took it and stood. He led her to the box of books that she'd effortlessly carried the day before.

"Would you be a good girl and lift this for me?" he said and pointed to the box.

When she failed to understand the meaning, he leaned over and tugged at the handles. She understood his request and tried but couldn't get the box off the ground. After a second attempt, she moved back to the couch, plopped down and returned to her book.

"Amazing," Hunter whispered. "Whatever the source of her strength, she can deplete it. I wonder how long it takes to build it back up?" He looked around and called out, "Mattie! We need food for the girl. Let's fill her up and see if that helps restore these abilities of hers."

"I don't know what to think about her." The words left my mouth as I slowly shook my head. "I just don't know…"

Chapter 6

For a city that had held over four and a half million people the previous year, London now served as home for just a couple of hundred thousand workers and government officials. It was still a respectable number, all things considered, and that population still required the daily items that made life possible, including the newspapers.

For the next three days, gallons of ink splashed across the newsprint, spoke of the fantastically strong woman and her act of heroism. Sketches of her and myself, thankfully none of which were very accurate, graced the front pages, while columns within the folds offered opinions on who she was and the possible dangers a super-powered human could present to polite society, especially in a time of war and unrest. But, without more sightings of the unearthly blond girl in the days following the bus mishap, the papers returned to the war news and mysuper powered guest fell out of the minds of the population.

Keely's education progressed at an alarming rate.

I kept my head in my work during the day while working with her in the evenings. Mattie spent her mornings teaching the young woman the letters of the alphabet and basic words. Their afternoons were spent cleaning and cooking. By the third week, she'd mastered the alphabet and the school's reading books. Although she still couldn't speak more than a handful of words in English, she'd already started writing basic words. Her penmanship was atrocious, but she had a certain knack at doodling. I'd find small sketches of Mattie, Dr. Hunter, and me along the edges of her writings.

Keely and I decided that afternoon walks should become a routine, despite the objections of Dr. Hunter and Mattie. I assured them that I'd keep her under control. There were risks but I knew that if she were to understand humanity, she needed to be out in the world, seeing it first-hand.

She was provided new dresses, almost daily since Mattie had plenty of unsold goods in her shop. Keely's fashion choices were driving poor Mattie insane. The older woman would drape Keely up in beautiful long dresses only to watch as she'd tear the sleeves off and rip the skirts, so they hung well above the knees. When we'd take the occasional stroll through the city, her beauty and wardrobe would turn heads and no doubt, stir up scandalous whispers among the few ladies that remained in town.

Each afternoon for the following two weeks, when her schooling and chores were done, I'd sit on the stool in my study, perched over my drawing boards and watch her through the window. Some days, the sunlight didn't appear through the blackened skies and she'd walk about pouting while studying the grass and trees. But when the golden rays struck the earth, she'd dance about with hands outstretched as if scooping the light from the air. It was those days that my work suffered from a lack of attention, but my heart soared.

When my work was done, we walked farther out into the neighborhoods of London. She marveled and dragged me around from sight to sight. The steambuses became a favorite attraction for Keely. We rode them all about town. Half the time, her head would be stuck out of the window like a puppy. She'd laugh and smile as the wind whipped her golden hair about.

It was the child-like innocence that both worried and enchanted me. Who was she, really? Where had she come from? Was there a reason for her appearance and what would that purpose be? And as selfish as it sounded to me, I worried about what would happen when her purpose was complete.

CRITICAL

I awoke realizing that it was three months to the day when Keely had fallen to Earth. When she'd fallen from the darkness, I'd been without much hope. I had been working hard on my latest weapon for the war effort, Henry the 8th, but knew that it wasn't the war winner the nation needed. A small part of me had already expected our eventual defeat.

And then she fell into my life bringing a sense of life and hope. Well, hope didn't come with her as much as she suddenly gave me a purpose again. Now, I was working to ensure that her life continued, and that my life continued so I could be at her side. For the first time in my life, I had met a woman with whom I wanted to spend the rest of my life. I didn't know if she had an interest in me, but I could hope. Maybe this was a foolish infatuation on my part. Still, I hoped for the best.

CRITICAL

Work progressed on Henry the 8th, slowly but surely. Keely frequently came into the workshop. After prancing around nude for the men on her second day here, they were eager for her to visit. But a stern lecture and warning about their behavior kept their tongues and wandering hands in check.

"What?" She asked and pointed to Henry.

At the moment, the spherical device seemed nothing more than a metal skeleton, a framework of orange painted aluminum. But all the components lay spread about on the workshop's tables. This was the first, a prototype, but if it worked, they'd be handing the schematics to the factories in the north for mass production. Since the isotopes were rare, mass production would mean only five or six devices a month.

I stepped beside her and answered, "This is Henry. He is a bomb." When I saw her face scrunch up in confusion, I threw my hands up and made an explosion sound. She nodded and I asked, "You know what a bomb is?"

She gave a stern look, "Yes. Me know."

Despite her expression, I couldn't help but smile. I just loved hearing her soft feminine voice. It'd only been the past couple of weeks that she had been speaking, but she was picking it up quickly.

"Thomas, why don't you take the rest of the afternoon off and show your lovely friend some more of the city," my workshop chief said as he stepped up behind me. "We've got everything we need. It's all a matter of putting it together and we've got the plans."

He gave me a hard pat on the back and leaned closer to whisper. "Look, you've been stuck in here for most of the week. Take it from me; if you leave a girl alone too long, she'll find 'er someone else who'll keep her company."

I thought about it and he was right. I'd had my head buried in my work for the past few days and could use some time outside. More importantly, I wanted, no, I needed time with her. My lab coat was tossed aside, and we left for a well-deserved afternoon stroll. At least, I thought it would just be a stroll.

Three hours later, we returned to my flat. Mattie stood in the center of the parlor, arms crossed and wicked gaze cast upon us. Dr. Hunter stood off to the side, but his demeanor wasn't much better.

Keely smiled and walked in as if nothing had happened. She moved sluggishly, having worn herself out.

I, on the other hand, smacked my lips and asked, "Should I take it that you two have already heard about this afternoon's events?"

"Tom," Hunter began with concern in his voice. "The Ministry of Defense sent someone here. Her actions have caught their attentions and someone in the crowd named you as her protector."

"Just what did the little missy do, anyways?" Mattie chimed in. "They said somethin' about her leapin' up and catching an airman."

"I took her for a walk and..." I started and watched as she walked out the back door and into the weak late afternoon sunlight. "We were at Victoria Park, walking up to the boating lake when we heard an air horn and sounds of propellers. One of the Navy's airships was coming over the city but was in distress. It was belching smoke and I could make out a fire in one of the engine houses. Without warning, there was a tremendous snapping and the whole ship jerked slightly."

I paused and remembered the way Keely had grabbed my arm at that moment, pointing, and so panicked that she forgot herself and rattled off words in her language.

"And then?" Hunter asked. I snapped back to the moment and continued.

"The keel had given, broken clean in two, I'd imagine." I noticed Mattie giving a questioning look. "Sorry, the keel on an airship is essentially its backbone. And with that severed, the vessel began to break in half, dropping in the center with the ends moving up like a jackknife closing."

"I heard the noise," Hunter said. "Didn't rightly know what the devil was happening, but that popping noise echoed all across London."

"Right. Well, the vessel was surely several hundred feet high as it began folding up. Keely pointed at it and shouted something. I didn't see it at first, but her eyesight appears to be far better than my own. I looked sharp but saw nothing at first but then something fell. A distant scream caught my attention and I knew some poor soul had slipped. His end was certain, but Keely grabbed my arm and shook me. She pointed and shouted something. I—I didn't know what to tell her. I mean, what was there to do except watch the man's demise or look away? And then it happened."

Mattie looked cross, "What happened?"

"I felt a blast of air and saw her streak upwards," I said and watched their faces twist in disbelief. "My hand to God, she shot straight up like a rocket and caught him. His momentum must have been great because she fell back to Earth once she had him but controlled their descent until they reached the ground at a leisurely pace, several feet from where I stood."

"How many people..." Hunter started but I stopped him.

"Scores of people were there and saw the whole event. But that isn't even the end, not even in the slightest. Once he was safely down, some in the crowd cried out and pointed to the wounded ship. We

56

were deafened by a series of creaks and groans as the metal framework began collapsing in on itself. The vessel was sinking in the sky and would have smashed into several tenement houses. And with that much hydrogen in its gasbags, the fire would have been immense, and God only knows what the death toll could have been."

"Could have been?" Mattie asked.

Nodding, I took a deep breath and considered the best words to describe what happened next. "In a blast of air and heat, she shot skyward again, latched herself to the underside of the vessel and, well for lack of a better explanation, she provided it with the lift required for it to remain airborne until it could make a safe landing, just outside the city." I paused and let the information settle. "She literally kept it aloft for over fifteen minutes, pushing it northward to the airfields. I remained there, uncertain what to do other than to avoid talking to anyone who voiced questions about her. When she finally returned half an hour later, we had to make a run for it. It took some doing, but we were finally able to shake off the pursuers who wanted to talk to her by darting through a couple of abandoned buildings, hiding for a while here and there, then taking a covered cab with the windows covered so no one could see us."

We stopped talking and walked into the kitchen.

There, through the windows, Keely danced and raced around the yard, playing in the intermittent rays of the sun.

"What do we do?" Mattie asked.

"The Ministry knows," Hunter's voice came out low and hushed. "It's a matter of time before they…"

"I don't know…" I replied. "If my work wasn't so essential, I'd ferry her out of the city until," I paused because I didn't know how to finish the thought. I looked at her again, running and playing in the sun's rays.

"Them government boys will be back," Mattie said. "How do we hide her?"

"Should we hide her?" Hunter replied and looked back and forth between us. He huffed at his own words. "Of course, we should."

Keely's face glowed with the innocent happiness that was usually only reserved for children as she danced in the back yard. I watched her and ignored the conversation between Mattie and Doctor Hunter. I couldn't let anyone take her away from me, but if the Ministry men returned, I wasn't sure I'd be given a chance to fight for her protection. I felt lost and uncertain of the future, but I took a deep breath and turned to my friends.

With conviction, I cut Mattie off mid-sentence. "We keep her here. We keep her safe. And we determine who and what she is."

"Are you sure?" Mattie asked. "If the Ministry think she is a…"

"Criminal? A creature from another world? Part of the Otherworlders' plans?" I said. "I don't know what or who she really is. All I know is, that one way or another, we've got to figure it out."

Chapter 7

Something changed between us on the first Sunday of her fourth month. We'd managed to hide Keely from the Ministry's men and our daily walks had been limited to the twilight hours, just in case anyone was watching. But today, I felt we'd be safe.

We sat side by side on a park bench during the late afternoon. She'd become restless after the daily shelling, as had I. Mattie packed a small but satisfying picnic and off we strolled. A tinge of guilt tugged at me. I'd left my men at the workshop to finish up some details on Henry the 8th, the nickname we'd given the new weapon I'd designed.

She darted away when sunlight fell around and she did her usual dance, catching it in her hands. I remember her eyes, so wide and innocent until the explosion rocked the city. A second and then a third followed, each preceded by a sharp whistling, the telltale sign of incoming enemy artillery shells.

I glanced around and saw massive plumes of smoke and fire belching up from behind us. A tenement building had taken a direct hit and from the looks of it, disintegrated completely. The brownstones on either side of it had partially collapsed. People ran to and fro, panicked, and unsure of what to do.

"Come on, we have to see if we can help," I yelled to her and we sprinted toward the destruction.

Within minutes, we arrived. I pointed to the rubble and shouted to her, "We've got to move as much as we can. There could be people trapped underneath."

Several other men charged into the piles of broken brick and wood. We struggled to move as much of the debris as possible, yelling out and listening for voices of the wounded calling back. Keely, on the other hand, show no signs of struggling as she lifted massive chucks of flooring and stonework and tossed them aside like they were made of paper.

The faster she worked, the more wounded we reached. Twelve broken and bleeding bodies were pulled from the remains of the structures. Glancing up, I saw Dr. Hunter kneeling over one of the injured, while others tended to the less wounded.

"I think that's everyone," one of the men said and I had to agree.

After digging for an hour, I was exhausted. I led

Keely over to the sidewalk where the wounded were still being cared for. The meat wagons had already transported most to the nearby hospital, but several still lay about.

"Damnit, I'm gonna lose him," Hunter exclaimed, and we rushed to his side. His left hand held tight against a spot on the wounded man's neck. Blood seeped through his fingers at an alarming rate. He glanced over his shoulder at us. "A splinter was lodged in his artery. I hoped to keep it there until we could get him to a proper surgeon. But the bloke had to feel around and yank it out."

"What do you need?" I asked, feeling lightheaded at the sight of so much blood.

"I need a finger on this spot so I can thread a needle. I think I have one in my bag." He said and nodded to the medical satchel, a few feet away.

"I don't think this is…" I started to say, but he knew of my aversion to blood and reached for Keely.

"Get down here," Hunter said as he snatched her hand and pulled her to her knees beside him. He yanked her closer and pushed her hand to the spot where his left hand rested. "I'm going to move my hand and you need to cover up the wound. Direct pressure." She resisted somewhat and he looked her in the eyes. "He will die. Do you understand what that means? All the blood will leave him if I can't sew him shut. Now," he pushed her hand hard against his and then slowly withdrew his bloody fingers and let hers fall against the seeping wound.

Her eyes widened and I saw the panic, the fear of not understanding, the fear of doing something wrong that could lead to a man's death. She did as she was told, but I saw the tears streaking down her face and the whimpering that escaped her. For the first time, I realized that she was truly frightened.

I knelt beside her, averting my eyes from the blood. My hand touched her chin and pulled her head around to look at me. I nodded and reassured her that she was doing well.

The procedure took several minutes, and Keely did her job, but I could see a change in her eyes. The concept of mortality may never have occurred to her. Once Dr. Hunter no longer needed her, she sat back and looked lost as she glanced at the dead and wounded. Her hands still dripped with blood and she held them close to her face, looking and sniffing. Tears welled up in her eyes and I could see the emotions churning. Horror and repulsion from the blood and gore were offset by the realization that her help had saved a human life. Wiping her hands clean, she looked over at me with uncertainty in her expression.

As Hunter worked, several men and I again dug

through the wreckage and pulled the remaining dead from beneath the shattered bricks and mortar. Exhausted now, I sat on a pile and just watched. She moved and sat beside me. Several folks in the crowd pointed and whispered about her. The newspaper headlines had been shouting her exploits, the bus, the airship, and more. I was too tired to care at the moment. Let them look and get it out of their system. My concerns were of a darker nature.

I slowly shook my head, "They've never hit us with anything like this before. If they can sustain an attack with a weapon like…" I paused and realized that she didn't need to hear any more.

An elderly couple sat nearby, and we watched the pair. The old man sat on the sidewalk, blood seeping from a deep gash on his forehead. The woman, his wife, sat next to him, turned toward him a little and pressed a cloth against his wound. Her tears were evident as they left streaks in the mortar dust that coated her cheeks and face. The woman's actions as she pushed herself close to him, held him, and kissed him proved that her tears were not of sadness but of joy that her love had not perished. We watched in silence as his arm slipped around her and his free hand cupped over hers.

I felt a touch on my hand, which rested on the stone beside me. I glanced down and saw that Keely's hand had moved and she slowly pushed it underneath mine. I looked up at her as my fingers curled around her small hand. Our eyes met and I saw my face reflected in hers.

She glanced to the couple and saw the woman kissing and nuzzling her face against her husband. She looked back to me, pushed herself close and placed a small kiss on my cheek. She pulled back slightly to gauge my reaction. The feel of her lips on my face sent shivers through me. I leaned forward and pressed my lips to hers. The first kiss was brief, as was the second, but the third I knew would last forever.

When we arrived home, a steamcar and courier from the Admiralty sat out front. The officer, a young man still cursed with pimples charged forward.

"Dr. Laybourne?" he asked, and I nodded. "I am charged with escorting you and the young lady to HQ. There is urgent business."

I glanced to Keely and then back to him. Somewhere inside, I knew it was only a matter of time.

"Are we under arrest?"

He shook his head. "No, Sir. I've only been

charged with collecting you."

I nodded to him and reached out for Keely. She took my hand into hers and looked at me, uncertain of what was transpiring. I gave her hand a reassuring squeeze.

"We'll come quietly."

Chapter 8

As we rode, my thoughts were a mishmash of concerns and worries. My mind simply refused to focus on any one detail. The new weapon, how many had fallen on London and the other southern cities, would I be punished for keeping Keely a secret, and most importantly, I worried about her safety.

I looked over at her. She had the window down and leaned her head out to feel the wind on her face. As she giggled, I silently prayed that she'd not be taken away from me.

We arrived and were escorted through one building and into another, then winding stairs down to what felt like the center of the Earth, and finally into a crowded meeting room. It would seem that we were the last to arrive.

The room was vast and open, with a ceiling that stretched up at least twenty feet. The whole of the room was paneled, and the walls were covered with maps, charts and assorted panels with papers affixed to them. The conference table stretched forty feet andwas lined with suited men and various military officers. Around the periphery, a dozen junior officers worried themselves about making sure that their leaders were afforded every possible convenience.

Our escort led us to a pair of empty chairs at the far end of the table. I pulled a seat out for Keely and I noticed her nervous glances around as she sat. Once I was seated, the senior officer and Admiral of the Fleet, Henry Fabb, addressed us.

"Dr. Laybourne, we missed you at the last meeting a few weeks ago, but your people have been keeping us abreast of your weapon's progress." Fabb leaned over the table, resting his elbows on it and cupping his cheeks in his hands. His eyes stared at Keely. "But it would seem there is more to your work than we first were told. Some kind of …" He waved to her but was at a loss for words.

I cleared my throat and stood. A sudden wave of nausea washed over me, but I kept myself in check. Military officers typically held men of science in low regard, unless, of course, those men were building a super weapon.

"I, umm … I'm sure that you've read the newspapers and heard the rumors about…" I motioned to Keely. "It's a long story but I've felt that it was best to try and determine who and what she was before bringing this matter to you."

The room erupted in noise. Every man wanted his opinion heard. Some called for her to be studied.

Others feared that she was a weapon of the enemy. After several minutes of shouts, Fabb silenced the room.

"As much as I'd like to discuss the girl, we have more pressing matters," he said as a short man ran up to him and whispered a message. He stood straight up and cleared his throat. "Gentlemen, the Queen is present."

Every man, including myself instantly jumped to our feet and bowed as the Queen, adorned in a simple white and gold dress, entered. She approached Fabb and said something that my ears could not make out. Looking suddenly pale, he stepped aside and allowed her to take his seat at the head of the table. With a wave, she motioned for everyone to take their seats.

She stared briefly at Keely before asking, "Is this the girl from the newspapers? The one they are calling 'super-human'?" I nodded and she continued. "Fascinating. She looks perfectly normal to me." There was a hushed murmuring around the table as every officer immediately agreed with the Queen's assessment of Keely. "Does she speak English?"

"She understands the spoken word, ma'am," I said and looked over at Keely. She appeared confused but looked back at me and smiled. "But she is still learning how to speak it correctly."

"Her exploits have the people chatting up a

storm." The Queen looked over at Fabb, "Do continue with your meeting."

He nodded and thanked her before addressing the room. "Two days ago, one of our airships passed over Wissant on the northern coast of France. The slugs have the largest collection of their long-ranged cannons positioned just west of the city's remains. A perfect place to target London, as well as all the other cities they shell daily; Canterbury, Brighton, Portsmouth, Southampton, just to name a few."

"I'd still like to know how they know where to shell. They've never been able to cross the Channel and as far as I know, they have no means of air travel," a naval officer asked abruptly.

One officer, a Royal Army field commander spoke up, "Good Lord, Jerry if these buggers have the intelligence to navigate the stars to Earth and the capabilities to lay waste to the armies of the Continent, I'd imagine that they'd know how to read a bloody French map."

Fabb cleared his throat and all eyes returned to him. "As I was saying, they do know where to hit us. So far, our only advantage has been that their long-range guns could only fire small shells that produced little damage. The scare tactic of a thirty-minute rain of shells on each city per day was enough to do the trick. But two days ago, our ship spotted something new. Six new weapons had been moved into place among the others. They appeared to be the same type of cannons, only several times the size. Today's shelling proved what they have become capable of doing to us. Six hits within London have left scores dead and caused a massive amount of property damage."

When the Queen spoke, everyone turned their attention to her. I was surprised at the softness in her voice, but the concern and worry were evident in her tone.

"Admiral, I've ordered the city emptied but we can't survive a prolonged assault from weapons of this type. Can't we just send a squadron of airships to bomb these guns?"

He looked at her and a smile appeared, "We can but it'll just be a temporary fix. Their gun emplacements have been frequent targets with mixed results. As soon as we knock a cannon out of action, they replace it. No, this time more drastic action is required." He looked directly at me. "That's why you're here, Dr. Laybourne. We need the Aspirium H8 device." He paused and gave a half smile. "We need your Henry."

It was as if all the air in my lungs disappeared. I swallowed hard as the attention of the room, and more notably, the Queen, turned to me. I tugged at my collar as I stood again.

"The device is in the final assembly stage. Once that is completed, we need a test firing to ensure that the weapon will work."

"Assembly, how long will that take?" Fabb asked.

"Umm, I could have the device ready for a test firing within two days' time," I replied and didn't like the look he gave me.

"And if we test fired this one, and it proves successful, how soon before we can have more?" he asked. The urgency in his tone was lost on no one in the room.

"If Henry works as planned and there are no major complications as a result of the explosion, we could have a second within two weeks. The munitions factories outside of the city could begin producing within two months," I replied and swallowed hard when the Queen spoke up.

"Henry?" she asked.

"I gave it a nickname during the design process and my team adopted it." I suddenly felt panic working its way through me. "Umm, H8 ... Henry the 8th."

She gave a grunt and smiled. "Seems appropriate to me. You said complications from the explosion, what does that mean?"

I looked at Fabb with concern. We'd already discussed the possibilities and I worried about stepping on toes with the answer. But he gave me a nod that I took as his approval to speak.

"The device uses isotopes that should produce an incredible amount of power, namely heat. Since we've never detonated something of this magnitude, we don't know what the result could be. There is a chance that the blast could ignite the atmosphere. If it did, the planet could be washed clean of all life."

She shifted uneasily in her seat, but I continued. "Regardless of what happens, it is a risk we must accept. If the slug's smoke factories continue, they will eliminate what little sunlight we still receive. That will destroy all plant life on Earth, meaning no farms, no crops, no food. We risk destroying the planet, or we surrender our world to them and allow our species to die off, slowly. Or worse, they'll will keep enough of us alive, perhaps in the tropical regions, to use as breeding stock. Just imagine, years after the fall of Earth, humans kept as animals; bred, contained on ranches or farms, and slaughtered for food. Much the way we have cattle and poultry farms, they'll keep their humans dumb, uneducated and docile."

The expression of shock on her face could not escape notice from everyone in the room. It seemed clear that the men in the room had not given her the full truth of what was to become of the human race in the days ahead. Their news had no doubt given her hope for victory. And then I had to open my mouth and speak the truth. A quick glance around the table confirmed that every uniformed man was glaring at me.

"No choice then?" she asked in a meek tone and I shook my head.

An awkward silence filled the room until Fabb spoke up, "Laybourne, we don't have time to do a test firing. In two days, we'll drop the bomb on the gun emplacements at Wissant. If it works, we'll eliminate a large number of their guns in one shot. They have others scattered about the French coast, but the bulk is at Wissant. Once Henry is unleashed, we're planning on a massive bombing campaign against the whole of Northern France. Bombing every gun site and all the ammo dumps. That'll buy us time to build more of your bombs without the shells raining on our cities."

"Sir, the goal of the H8 program was to drop them on the smoke factories since conventional bombings had yielded nothing," I said. "One bomb can't..."

"Things have changed. The cannons are not the only things we've spotted in Wissant. They are constructing a flotilla of vessels and amassing a landing force," He said. "Things have changed, Dr. Laybourne. We've never seen them building barges or boats before. They're adapting. This is about our long-term survival. This is about preventing an invasion of our isles. If Henry works the way you initially proposed it would, this will change everything and give us the turning point in this struggle we so desperately need."

D. Alan Lewis

Chapter 9

"You're going where?" Mattie and Dr. Hunter shouted in unison.

I sighed in despair and explained again, "The Admiralty has requested, no … ordered me to travel on board the airship that will drop Henry. I'm to make sure the bomb is prepared properly before deployment and then observe the effects after detonation."

"And you're taking her because…?" Mattie asked, waving her hand toward the rear of the house.

I looked out the back window at Keely as she danced and chased the sunlight. "The Queen was rather taken with her exploits, just as the people seems to be. After the official meeting ended, the officers made it known that they want to put her to use."

"What kind of use?" Hunter asked.

"Since the people are fascinated with her, they mean to use her to bolster the war effort. Make her poster girl for the Empire's struggle. If the bomb works, the higher-ups mean to invade the Continent and reclaim it for the Crown," I said and looked again at her. "Mattie, since she is going to be a poster girl, can you design something for her to wear? Something patriotic and inspiring."

Mattie nodded and stepped to the table. In short order, she'd begun sketching out ideas. Dr. Hunter chattered on for a bit about the war efforts and the foolish notion of retaking Europe alone. I just tuned out his words as I watched Keely dance. But something, an unclear thought, began to form in my mind. It was a notion at first, but the more I watched her, the more I started to realize the truth of it all."

"Sun light…" I whispered and didn't respond to Hunter immediately when he asked what I meant. "Don't you see? The missing ingredient is sunlight. That first day, when she fell," I paused and thought back to her arrival, trying to ensure I was correct "That first day, a ray of light came into the room. She'd not stirred until that moment. Each time she uses these abilities, she is weakened, but then she chases the rays of the sun around, bathing her hands in the light. She is absorbing it. Of course, how could I have been so blind!" I slapped myself on the forehead, certain I was right.

I looked at him and saw the confusion. I could appreciate his disbelief, but I was certain I was correct.

"Think about it like this. A plant uses sunlight to

complete the process of photosynthesis. She does something similar. That's why she was naked when she fell and why she keeps tearing all her clothes off, or at least ripping portions of them off to expose her limbs. She is baring as much of her skin as she can to collect the sun's energy."

Hunter slowly nodded and I could see the wheels turning as he considered the implications of what I was telling him. After a moment, he spoke in a hushed tone. "That would make sense. Why she could lift that God-awful heavy box of books one day and after wearing herself out with that airship, she couldn't. My God—do you understand the ramifications of this? Part of me had scoffed at the idea of her actually being from another world. But she is. She has to be." We both glanced out the window at her. "And she fell to Earth to…?"

"Save us?" I muttered. "To inspire us to continue. That's what the Queen wants her to do."

"My boy," Hunter's voice shook slightly as he continued. "While I know the Queen has designs on her to be used as a symbol of hope and strength, her abilities—well, I mean, she…" He paused and I turned to face him.

"You think someone sent her here as a weapon?" I asked and he nodded. I straightened up as the images of her on the battlefield passed through my mind's eye. "No. I can't allow her to be in that kind of danger. A symbol? Yes. A warrior? No."

I rushed to Mattie's side and looked at her drawings. She'd sketched out a nice dress with a flowing long skirt. It was totally unacceptable. I knew that Keely would immediately rip the skirt and the sleeves away.

I snatched the pencil from her hand and made some alterations. "No, Mattie. Let's shorten the skirt to here. This is about where she usually rips them up to anyway. And the top … let's do away with the sleeves and open the front down to here. It may show more cleavage than fashionable, but we'll have to make do and her midriff should be bare."

"You might as well have the little tart naked as the day she were born," Mattie said and scooted her chair back from the table in a show of defiance. "I'll tell you this, I ain't making an outfit like this. It's positively scandalous."

I glared at her for a moment and then struck on an idea that would bring her to my way of thinking.

"Yes, this is revealing, but you just heard what we were saying about her abilities. Her skin collects the sunlight. She needs to have as much skin showing so as to collect the maximum amount. Besides that…" I stooped beside her and looked into her gray eyes. "If she is the Empire's poster girl for the war effort, everyone and I mean everyone will see her and see the clothing she's wearing. Imagine being able to say that her clothing was made at Warner's Dressmakers and that you were her personal clothing designer. If I'm correct, despite her scandalous attire, every woman in the Empire will want to mimic her style. Especially young women, who always look to the royals or celebrities for their fashion standards. Imagine how many people will flock to the dressmaker of Britain's newest heroine. No—the world's newest heroine."

Her eyes lit up at the prospect. I could almost see the fires in her imagination being stoked. She nodded and took to redesigning Keely's new look.

"I can do all the compromises you want but I want to give her a cape," she said and looked up at me. "Something to wrap around herself when needed … for modesty's sake."

"Wait here," I said and dashed from the room only to return moments later with a bundle of cloth in my hand. "Use this."

She looked up at the Union Jack, the one I'd wrapped her up in on the day she fell.

"A Jack?" she twisted up her face.

"If she is going to be a patriotic symbol, why not wrap her up in the very symbol of England and the Empire itself," I said and looked out the window at

Keely as she danced. "Let's make her the hero that this nation needs. We may die in the end, but let's leave this world with hope in our hearts."

ଓଃ୫୦୦ୡ୫୦

As Mattie sewed, I spent the rest of the day and the next pushing my men to finish construction of Henry the 8th. The task required my constant attention and my time with Keely suffered. She came to the workshop, randomly during the day and evening, but would become bored as the men and I struggled to cram months of work in the forty-eight short hours.

When I saw her pout and walk away, my heart shuddered and sank. I didn't want to deny myself to her, but the work had to be done. Occasional blasts throughout the city from the Otherworlders' newer canons constantly reminded me of the importance of what we were trying to accomplish. I only hoped she understood.

For all her power, I couldn't help but think of her as a grown child. I didn't know her true age, but like a youngster, she was trying to find her way in this big, strange world. There were emotions that conflicted with the realities of the world, my emotions and her's, alike.

As we buttoned up the last panel, I uttered a silent prayer asking for Divine intervention. I'd built the most destructive force known to man. And now, I didn't care of it saved the world. I only wanted it to save her.

೮೩೮೦೮೩೮೦

Certain that the weapon was ready, I lay in bed that evening and contemplated the coming events. We'd be transported to the airfields outside of town, the bomb would be loaded, and we'd depart. And after that, most of the morning would be spent in the air until our target was reached. And then...

"Thomas?" Her voice, barely a whisper resonated through the darkness.

I cleared my throat and sat up. In the doorway, I could just make out her silhouette against the flickering glow of the downstairs fireplace that shown up through the stairway and illuminated the hall. She moved into the room, letting her nightgown drop in the process.

Without thinking, I scooted to the side as she slipped into the bed next to me. Guilt gnawed at me briefly, but the feel of her flesh against mine eradicated all doubts that my actions and intentions were wrong. My head dropped back to the pillow as she laid hers on my chest and pushed herself against me. I wanted her, needed her in the worst way, but that wasn't why she had come to me.

Content, she nuzzled her face against my neck and let her hand move to my chest, where she found contentment running her fingers through the light patch of fur there. I turned slightly and kissed her head, over and over. The rush from each one never diminished.

It didn't take long before her eyes closed, and she fell asleep. My eyelids were heavy, and sleep was taking me, but I held onto consciousness as long as possible. I didn't want the moment to end. I didn't want to lose the sensation of her flesh against mine, the feel of the heat of her body warming me and listening to the rhythmic sound of her breathing.

And then the fear set in, fear of losing her to the enemy or worse, having the government take her away. I kissed her once more before I closed my eyes and mouthed the words to her that I didn't have to courage to say out loud.

Chapter 10

It'd been designated R178 when christened but the airship was known to its crew as '*Firebrand*'. Since the war began, the shipyards had churned out vessels like this one at an alarming rate. Each class usually had a dozen or so built before improvements were added along with an increase in size. The *Firebrand* was roughly the size of an old sea-going battleship, with a few cannons that could fire down at an enemy along with a tremendous bomb payload. When unleashed, over a hundred bombs could rain down on a target. The problem we were encountering was that the slugs had developed anti-airship guns that could bring down an air-going vessel if they hit it enough times. Or worse, if they hit it once in the right spot with an incendiary round. More than a few vessels had exploded and burnt to ash as they fell.

In order to avoid their fire, our airships had to fly higher than the slugs' guns could shoot. Height meant safety but with it, came the drawbacks. Bombing accuracy was almost nonexistent. Our bombing attacks were like shooting a quail with a scattergun. A few pellets may hit, but the majority wouldn't come close, spread out over a far-ranging area.

I watched Keely walk around the wooden decks, looking over the railings and watching the world pass under us. Her new outfit kept my eyes, as well as the crews', occupied, despite our best attempts to be gentlemen.

Mattie's creative flair had proven to be to Keely's liking. Her pleated navy-blue skirt only dropped down enough to cover the upper third of her thighs and was held in place with a maroon belt and sparkling brass buckle. Her white blouse lacked sleeves but the edges and plunging neckline were trimmed with lace. The top was cut obscenely short, just covering her breasts, and leaving her midriff bare. Attached on the back of it was the cape. Just as I'd asked, Mattie had fashioned the Union Jack perfectly. The final touch was a pair of short red boots with brass trimmings.

As I stepped onto the control deck, the ship's commander shouted out, "Take her up 'nother hundred yards. Gotta make sure we're out range of their gun."

Another man repeated the order and I watched as the command crew sprang to life. A wheelman spun the massive control wheel, adjusting the elevators on the rear of the vessel. I felt my stomach lurch as *Firebrand's* nose rose. Grabbing a nearby railing, I steadied myself as the ship tilted up for a short jaunt and then leveled off.

Captain Hicks, a man about my age turned and looked me over. The man had a few inches on me, but I had a few pounds on him, which didn't set well with me. Maybe a little too much of Mattie's cooking over the past few months had clung to my midsection.

Hicks's voice conveyed his concerns as he spoke. "Doctor Laybourne, a question about this bomb of yours. I was given the particulars about it before leaving, however those particulars were rather vague. What altitude should we be at when it is dropped? Just how big of an explosion are you really expecting?"

"I'm not certain, but we should be safe at this height." I lied. Truth be known, I had no idea of what would really happen. "And as for the particulars being vague, I'm afraid I can't tell you much either. The weapon hasn't been test fired, so we're not certain of the true nature of the blast it will produce."

He narrowed his eyes. "But you are certain that we'll be safe at this height?" I kept my expression blank and slowly nodded. He scrunched up his face and I could see he understood the dilemma. "Understood, Doctor. Understood."

A crewman chimed out from the foreword section of the deck, "Coming up on the coast,

Captain." He lowered the binoculars and looked back at us with a smile. "I see the guns. This should be quite a show."

"Please remember to have your men put on their goggles shortly before we release Henry," I reminded the Captain. "The flash from the explosion could be damaging to the eyes."

He nodded, "I doubt a flash would affect the *Eagle*."

A few miles behind us, the *Eagle*, one of *FireBrand's* sisterships, cruised along. It matched our speed and altitude but would remain a few knots behind us to make sure they were not damaged. It would act as an observer for the attack and then fly over and inspect the damage should we be unable to do so. A series of newly developed cameras with long-ranged lenses lined *Eagle's* lower deck. The photographs would be invaluable to the Admiralty, showing the blast radius, effects and what, if anything, survived.

The sounds of muffled explosions caught my attention. The crew seemed unconcerned, but the Captain took note of my jumping at each boom. While Keely and some other men ran to the railings and looked down on the distant weapons, I found I was happier staying in the center of the deck. Sometimes I hated being such a coward.

The Captain glanced over at me and gave a reassuring nod. "They're firing shells at us. They're set to detonate at certain altitudes, but their guns can't lob a round above 2500 feet and we're cruising at 3500, so we're safe. They'll just blow up harmlessly underneath us."

"What about the shrapnel?" I asked.

He shook his head. "The blasts can't push the stuff up this high. We'll be safe. Don't worry, Doctor. The Air Navy will get you there and back. We've seen a fair amount of combat since the old girl was launched two years ago. *FireBrand* is the most decorated air vessel in—history. You're in good hands, Doctor."

Keely ran to me, grabbed my arm, and pointed to the edge of the deck where she'd been standing. "Look!"

With some reluctance, I let her pull me to the edge of the deck and glanced down at the green and blue scene. Directly below us, the line between land and sea passed. I looked up and saw the guns in the distance. They appeared tiny, like little black twigs that sparked on the tips each time a new payload was released in our direction. And below us, the occasional burst of AA rounds puffed out fire then quickly expanded into a puffy black cloud.

"We're safe up here. The Captain has assured

me," I said, hoping to calm her, but I didn't feel very certain of it, myself.

Looking down again and squinting slightly, I could make out the fleet of barges. The ships lined the coast along a large inlet, squeezed together so tightly that they appeared to be joined from this distance. A little way from the sea, I could see encampments. This must be the invasion force Admiral Fabb spoke about. I winced at the size. There could easily be thousands of them, waiting for the chance to spread their destruction across our isle.

We jumped as another wave of AA fire blasted around the ship. But when razor-sharp metal ripped the deck open a matter of feet from us, I knew something had gone terribly wrong. I grabbed her hand and pulled her into the interior of the flight deck.

The ship shuddered as more shots struck nearby. The sound of metal shrapnel raining across the decks and structure caused the crew to scramble. The Captain shouted orders for more altitude while others yelled about damage to various sections of the ship. The flight deck suddenly became a confusing cacophony of shouting men, clanging metal, and the groaning of the ship as its nose arched up, yearning for more height.

"Fire!" Someone shouted. "Aft bags."

Captain Hicks yelled for the CO2 tanks to be dumped in that area and looked at me. "Apparently they have new AA guns in addition to the new cannons. I'm not sure we'll make it to the drop point at a safe height."

The nose began pitching up again and I could feel the deck drop slightly. The ship was slowly losing its battle against gravity and began dropping.

"Understood." I said to the Captain and held Keely close as another volley of AA fire erupted around us.

The forward two gas bags, filled with deadly hydrogen, were torn open, leaking the lighter-than-air gas. Divine intervention prevailed on our part and the gas didn't ignite. The nose dropped and the ship began to plummet toward Earth. I struggled to hold her and stand upright but when she shouted at me, I understood. It wasn't that she was trying to stay on her feet, Keely wanted free. I opened my arms and let her go. In an instant, she darted to the deck's edge and shot into the air.

Circling underneath, Keely positioned herself and I could hear her yells as she struggled to push against the vessel. Although we still dropped, the rate slowed. It was just as I'd seen her do in London. She controlled our descent and kept *Firebrand* reasonably level.

Several more AA shots hit, ripping the remaining bags open. By the time we hit the ground, Keely was the only thing generating lift for the vessel.

The impact with the French countryside knocked me to the wooden planks of the deck. I remained still for short time as gunfire erupted from around us. A few of the braver crewmen, who'd stood up, were immediately riddled with bullets from the Otherworlders' weapons.

I heard someone from behind me and looked back. One of the bombardiers entrusted with Henry, crawled frantically to the Captain. Occasional shots smacked against the ship, forcing us to remain as flat as possible. Keely landed on the far side of the ship and casually strolled to me. Several bullets struck her and simply bounced off as if she were made of steel. I held out my hand and pulled her down, drawing her closer to me for protection. I was not sure if I was trying to protect her, or if she was trying to protect me, but either way, I was happy to have her with me.

"Captain, Doctor, the bomb! I was prepping it for the drop. The fuses were already in place before the ship was hit. When we crashed the detonator's countdown started. We got minutes," he reported frantically.

I looked into her eyes and saw the exhaustion within her. What power she had must have be drained in an effort to control our crash. My sweet Keely was almost powerless.

The boom of a cannon followed by a deafening explosion on the rear of the ship made us all duck and cover our heads. In the distance, unearthly shouts from the slugs could be heard. Cheers and yells erupted from their lines. They'd downed an airship and meant to exact some measure of revenge for our constant bombings.

I raised my head a bit and looked out. All around the remains of the airship the Otherworlders advanced. Seeing them in person for the first time, I realized that the boasts of their size and repulsiveness hadn't been exaggerated. Humanoid in shape, they stood a dozen feet tall. Their heads lacked noses and ears like a human but held four eyes. Their grayish skin glimmered in the way that a reptile's body would in the sunlight, not slimy but slick-looking.

When the slugs had advanced to a hundred feet or so of *Firebrand,* several of the crew opened fire with rifles. Six slugs fell on the first volley. Seeing that we weren't going down without a fight, they halted their advance and crouched in defensive stances.

"We're doomed," I said, looking into her eyes. "The bomb will detonate in minutes. It'll wipe out every living thing for who knows how far."

She shook her head and stood. In a defiant tone she said, "No, Thomas Laybourne. We survive."

With that said, she walked across the deck and jumped to the ground. Captain Hicks barked some orders to his men, but I was too focused on her to know what was said.

She marched forward, toward the closest group of slugs. One Otherworlder, dressed in elaborate armor and headdress moved out from their line, as if to challenge her. He was obviously their leader or a high-ranking officer, assuming they had a chain of command like human militaries do.

She'd gotten halfway to him when the slug raised a hand and shouted something. Immediately, the guns behind him fired off. I saw the rounds striking her and in her weakened state she couldn't completely resist them. The large bullets smashed into her, knocking her back a few steps, but she refused to fall.

The lead slug scoffed and shouted something in his tongue. A mighty roar arose from the many others behind him. He waved, and in no time a deafening roar of a mechanical nature sounded out from behind them. Over a slight rise, a metal vehicle moved toward her. Like the slugs, it was huge and heavily armored. Massive tracks on either side provided the traction needed to move the giant vehicle over any terrain. It sported a massive cannon the size of a tree trunk on a rotating turret which sat atop the main body of the metal behemoth.

Keely stopped when she saw it and glanced back at me. I could see the fear in her eyes. I started to jump down and run to her, but the Captain's hand grabbed my arm.

"Don't be a fool," he whispered. "You'll be shot to hell."

The lead slug held up a three-fingered hand and then brought it down to point straight at her. The cannon on the mechanized vehicle fired. I could feel the report in my chest and felt the heat from the firing as well as the detonation across every inch of me.

The shell hit her square in the chest and exploded. The blast deafened me and for a moment, all I could see were spots. When my vision cleared, Keely lay a dozen feet back from where she'd been. Her arms and legs were motionless, and I couldn't see any signs of life from her until her head rolled slightly. Her costume was scorched, and thin ribbons of smoke rose from the burnt material. My frozen heart began beating again, seeing that she lived through the attack, but in her weakened state, I wasn't sure if she'd survive another hit like that.

I want to say that it was bravery, chivalry, or some other nonsense such as that, which caused my next actions, but it wasn't. It was my own selfishness.

It was my needs, not hers, that pushed me to act.

I leapt from the wreckage and ran to her, sliding in the loose soil until I was at her side. I covered her body with my own, in hopes that I could protect her in some manly way. But deep down, it was a fear of losing her that hurt me the most. As much as I wanted to protect her, I needed to be the first to die, because I couldn't stomach the notion of a world without her in it. Even if my life ended minutes or seconds later, the idea that I'd be forced to witness her death tore at my soul. I would die, at their hands or the firestorm that my bomb would bring, but I would die protecting her. I would die knowing that she still lived, for a short time after my death, anyway.

I looked back at the laughing slugs. They howled at the sight. A puny human protecting the woman he loved. The woman he'd loved since the first moment his gaze fell upon her.

As I turned back to her, something caught my eye. An idea, born of desperation came to me. I lightly slapped her cheek until she stirred. When her eyes met mine and I saw the spark of life within her, I lifted her weak body and ran.

The bullet, fired from a random slug's rifle, grazed my left thigh and I stumbled. Seeing that I wouldn't reach my objective, I pushed her away and threw her as I fell. I hit the ground hard, as did she.

"Keely!" I said and saw her look at me.

I pointed to the ground, a few feet from her. She turned and saw what I'd desperately tried to reach, a patch of sunlight that fell upon the scorched ground, a few feet away. She struggled to crawl and stretched her hand out until the rays hit her. Hearing the slugs roaring with laughter at the spectacle, I turned and pulled myself up. She needed time, time to absorb as much as possible. I only hoped she could fly far away before the bomb detonated.

"You big ugly brutes," I yelled. "Are you too weak to kill an unarmed civilian? We may be smaller than you… we may lack the science you possess, but we will resist with every fiber of our being. You may have rolled over the Russians, the Germans, the Americans, the French, and countless others, but you have yet to deal with the likes of us. You may take our isle, but you will be made to suffer for every inch of British soil you claim."

A cheer arose from the crew of *Firebrand*. I hadn't expected it but welcomed the distraction since the slugs were looking back and forth between me and the crashed vessel. Keely, it seemed wasn't a concern to them at the moment. So much the better, I thought.

The lead slug sneered. I didn't think he could understand my words. It was the notion that I was being defiant that annoyed him. Something about that pleased me greatly.

He raised a hand and shouted something. The others behind him rose and aimed their weapons at me. My chest tightened and I found I couldn't breathe. This was it. I would die, but she still had a chance. The smile felt right as I thought about her streaking away to safety. I didn't see myself being heroic. I was just a fool, in love with a woman who fell from the sky.

The moment his hand dropped; I heard the reports of the rifles but felt nothing. I opened my eyes to see Keely standing in front of me. Her body shielded me from their fire. As the slugs roared again with anger, she turned to me.

"Keely, thank you, but you have to go. The bomb is ticking. It has seconds left by this point. Fly quick and true and you'll be safe," I said in a pleading manner.

She tilted her head and smiled. In a blurring dash, she left me. But instead of fleeing, she tore into the airship's remains and exited seconds later with the massive bomb in her hands. Switching positions, she held the structure of the weapon with one hand and began spinning. Like a child's top, she spun until all of her features, as well as the bomb's, blended together. Then the image tilted and in a blast of wind and sound, she released Henry the 8th.

The massive bomb shot skyward, straight up until I lost sight of it. The slugs didn't speak or fire upon us, apparently as mesmerized by her actions as I was. Realizing that the blast was seconds away, I shouted to the airship's crew.

"Cover your eyes!"

The explosion produced a blinding flash that made my eyes, even though they were covered by my hands, see spots. A minute later, the shockwave hit us, knocking the breath from my lungs, and deafening me. The last thing I heard before my ears rang were the many screams from the slugs, blinded by the unexpected light. I could only imagine that most were still watching Henry's climb when the isotopes fused and ignited.

Dazed, I stood and looked about. The Captain and crew stepped into the open, looking skyward. When I turned to the slugs, they were holding their eyes and staggering about. With four eyes, the flash would have affected them more.

They screamed and squealed in pain, covering and rubbing their ruined eyes. And then I looked at her and saw the light. She was drenched in the light, as was the ground around her.

Looking up, the spherical fireball shrank, but the bigger effect was still under way. Henry's blast had produced an atmospheric shockwave that spread out in all directions, like the waves on water when disturbed by a tossed rock. The shockwave pushed the black clouds away, opening the heavens above. Sunlight, not seen in this force in many months, fell upon the Earth again for miles around us.

When I looked back to her, Keely's arms were stretched out and her head thrown back. Her skin soaked in the abundant light and in short order, began to glow. Her feet left the ground as she rose and hovered a couple of feet above the scorched dirt. With each passing moment, the glow of her flesh grew brighter. What little scorched clothing still clung to her form, smoked briefly before disappearing in a flash of brilliant flames. Free of obstruction, her body soaked up even more of the rays and I realized that her powers were growing beyond measure. She wasn't just stronger and tougher than a human, she was a goddess. Keely, like a flower, blossomed before our eyes into her true self, the superhero, for lack of a better term, she was meant to be.

She looked at me and pointed to the airship, "Get inside. Be safe. I handle the slugs." When I hesitated, she dashed to me and looked into my eyes. "Please. Be safe."

"Whatever you do. Whatever happens, I want you to know that … I love you." I confessed and saw her radiant lips curl up into a smile.

When I stepped back toward the wreckage, she bit her lip and nodded. "Thomas Laybourne, Keely love you." My heart soared as she smiled.

She shot skyward briefly, almost disappearing out of sight before slamming down like a lightning bolt into the mechanized vehicle. The thing exploded violently, peppering the slugs around it with debris. From the cloud of smoke, she shot out and rocketed a few feet above the ground, slamming into slugs and their weapons.

"She's giving us a chance, boys," the Captain shouted. "They're still blinded from the blast. Open up on 'em"

The slugs ran to and fro trying to stay out of Keely's way, but now found themselves under fire from the *Firebrand's* crew. The confused aliens staggered about, blinded and stunned. They were easy targets for Keely and the guns of the crew.

A cannon blast behind me startled me badly. I turned to see that *Firebrand's* crew had jumped up to man two of the ship's three-inch cannons. Their shells began raining destruction on the slugs, blasting bodies and pieces of Otherworlders, skyward.

I dashed into the wreckage and watched Keely go. Plumes of smoke arose from the slug's massive cannons as she destroyed each one with ease. When she flew overhead, I darted to the backside of the wreckage and watched her streak across the sky, toward the anchored barges along the coast. Keely circled around and shot straight at the side of the farthest vessel, so close to the waterline that her flight whipped the water into the air. She slammed into the barge, passing straight through into the next. One by one, the barges jerked violently as she tore through each one until she'd punctured through the entire line. Before she had gone through the last one, the first had already sunk below the dark waters of the channel.

When they first arrived, no human force had stood their ground against the slugs. Their victories were complete, brutal, and had been achieved quickly, without loss to themselves. For the first time, they found themselves on the opposite side of that kind of battle. They were outnumbered by a single girl.

And she never appeared to grow tired. Despite the amount of power she used in her attacks, the sunlight continued to feed her the necessary energy to remain the dominate force in the fight. By the end, Keely was on her feet, striking down the Otherworlder soldiers, one at a time.

Chapter 11

I sat in my study and sketched out a new idea for the latest airship. It'd be bigger than the last class, stronger and better armored against the Otherworlders' AA guns. I knew that my focus should be on the project, but as she always did during the mid-afternoon, Keely drew my attention from the papers. With the second anniversary of the Battle of Wissant approaching, the Queen planned a major celebration with Keely and myself as honored guests. I knew I'd lose another week of work as a result of the ceremonies and appearances, but one does not deny the Queen a reason to throw a party or two.

I laid my pen down and leaned back in my chair, keeping my eyes on her. Keely danced about in the backyard in her favorite white dress. By Mattie's standards, it was obscenely short and showed far too much skin, but that wasn't anything new.

Upon word of our victory, our factories began churning out more of the isotope bombs, Henry's cousins, as we called them. One by one, the smoke factories in Europe were destroyed, completely and totally by the intense fires generated by the disruption and smashing of atoms. Keely and I flew with each bomb, ensuring its arrival.

Our victory at Wissant was just a small wave that had begun a tsunami of human resistance. The war still raged on, but with the continent cleared of their factories, the skies over Britain were now mostly free of the black smoke. Sunlight, along with hope, had returned to our isle.

We found allies throughout the globe. Japan, Cuba, and many other island nations had been spared invasion by the slugs. Using them as staging points, the Empire fought back to reclaim the fallen nations of humanity. Pockets of resistance were found across the scorched lands of Europe and North America. Supply runs of food and weapons kept them alive and fighting. Every nation on the globe was locked in the struggle to reclaim the Earth as ours.

The Admiralty had not been pleased with me when I insisted that Keely retire from the war effort for a few months, but when the Queen heard the joyous news she put her foot down and took up my cause. Someone, early on after the battle, had claimed Britain would need an army of super-humans like Keely.

The notion still makes me chuckle to this day. I

ran my hands through my hair and resigned myself to the knowledge that I'd get no more work done today. Instead, I stared out at her like I always do. The first hints of a baby bump showing through the thin cotton material reminded me to never give up hope. She and I would not produce an army, instead we'd start a family.

With the daily sunlight providing a constant stream of power, she didn't need to be outside as much, chasing down the few spots of sunlight like she needed to before. Still, she loves to sway in the light and I never tire of watching her out there, in the back yard, dancing in the sun.

About the Author

In 1965, an object fell from space, somewhere near Kecksburg, PA. This was the same year that Alan was born. To date, no connection has been made between the two events but that hasn't stopped the conspiracy theorists and his family from speculating,

D. Alan Lewis is an 'alleged' native of Chattanooga, Tennessee who resides in Nashville with a fish name Wolfgang.

You can follow Alan at www.dalanlewis.com
Or on Facebook: Author-D-Alan-Lewis
Or on Twitter: @Dalanlewis

If the paranormal is your game, check out **www.voodoorumors.com** for a noir detective series with a twist.

GUNFIGHTS, AIRSHIPS AND BULLET-PROOF CORSETS ARE JUST PART OF THE JOB FOR AMERICA'S PREMIERE STEAMPUNK SPIES.

THE LIGHTNING BOLTS OF ZEUS

BOOK 1 OF THE HAWKE GIRLS' ADVENTURES

BY D. ALAN LEWIS

AVAILABLE ON AMAZON.COM OR YOUR LOCAL BOOK SELLER.

D. Alan Lewis

The Blood Red Ruby

Voodoo Rumors 1951

One gem, five men, forty-eight hours of non-stop terror.